ORPHEUS AND EURYDICE

IN MEMORY OF MICK MORDEN (1934–2007) AND
NANCY MILLER (1953–2012) — H. L. AND D. M.

TO NINA AND NOAH — C. H.

● ● ● ● ● ● ● ● ●

PRONUNCIATION GUIDE

Apollo . . . . uh-PAUL-oh
Cerberus . . . . KER-ber-us
Charon. . . . . CARE-on
Eurydice. . . . . yur-RID-uh-see
Fates. . . . . FAYTZ
Hades. . . . . HAY-deez

Lesbos . . . . LEZ-boss
lyre. . . . . LIE-er
Orpheus. . . . . OR-fee-us
Persephone . . . . per-SEH-fon-ee
pyre . . . . PIE-er

● ● ● ● ● ● ● ● ●

BIBLIOGRAPHY

Calasso, Roberto. *The Marriage of Cadmus and Harmony*. New York: Vintage, 1994.
Graves, Robert. *The Greek Myths*. London: Pelican Books, 1955.
———. *The White Goddess: A Historical Grammar of Poetic Myth*. London: Faber & Faber, 1948.
March, Jenny. *Cassell's Dictionary of Classical Mythology*. London: Cassell Reference, 1998.
Ovid. *Metamorphoses*. Translated by Mary Innes. London: Penguin, 1955.
Schwab, Gustav. *Gods and Heroes*. New York: Pantheon, 1974.

● ● ● ● ● ● ● ● ●

Barefoot Books
2067 Massachusetts Ave
Cambridge, MA 02140

Text copyright © 2013 by Hugh Lupton and
Daniel Morden
Illustrations copyright © 2013 by Carole Hénaff
The moral rights of Hugh Lupton, Daniel
Morden and Carole Hénaff have been asserted

First published in the United States of America
by Barefoot Books, Inc in 2013
All rights reserved

Graphic design by Ryan Scheife,
Mayfly Design, Minneapolis, MN
Color separation by B & P International,
Hong Kong
Printed in China on 100% acid-free paper
This book was typeset in Agamemnon,
Dante MT Std and Mynaruse
The illustrations were prepared in acrylics

ISBN 978-1-84686-784-2

Library of Congress Cataloging-in-Publication
Data is available under LCCN 2012011236

1 3 5 7 9 8 6 4 2

ORPHEUS
— AND —
EURYDICE

RETOLD BY HUGH LUPTON & DANIEL MORDEN

ILLUSTRATED BY CAROLE HÉNAFF

Barefoot Books

step inside a story

Contents

CHAPTER ONE

A WEDDING AND A FUNERAL

THERE HAS ONLY BEEN ONE mortal man whose skill at playing the lyre compared with that of the god of music, golden Apollo.

His name was Orpheus. When he played, the birds would swoop down from the heavens and perch on the branches above his head. When he played, the animals of the fields would gather around him, their heads cocked to one side as they listened to him. It was said that when he played even the trees would dance. Have you ever seen trees standing in circles and avenues? It is said that those are the places where Orpheus stopped playing before the dance was finished. In those places we can still see the patterns of the dance.

Now, Orpheus had fallen in love with a woman called Eurydice. There was a wedding, a magnificent wedding with many guests and delicious food to eat. All the master musicians were there, playing instruments of every kind.

But all through the wedding ceremony the candles and lamps in the temple gave off an oily black smoke, so that the guests coughed and choked. Even the priests had to wipe tears from their eyes. They looked at one another and shook their heads. "This is a bad omen," they said. "Such things should never happen at a wedding."

The priests had good reason to be worried.

The morning after the wedding, Eurydice woke up early. She climbed out of bed while Orpheus was still deep in sleep. She pulled on her clothes and slipped outside.

Dawn was breaking. The warm autumn light woke a snake that was coiled up on a rock. It slid through the grass just as Eurydice was stepping barefoot across the meadow. Their paths crossed. Startled, the snake sank its fangs into Eurydice's ankle. Its poison coursed through her veins. With a cry she fell to the ground.

When Orpheus found her, she was lying dead and cold in the dew-damp grass. He lifted her in his arms. He carried her home, his face wet with tears.

And so it came about that the day after their wedding was the day of Eurydice's funeral. The wedding guests, who the day before had gathered in joy, now gathered in sorrow as her body was laid on a pyre, piled high with wood.

Coins were placed over her eyes to pay the ferryman who would carry her across the water to the Land of the Dead. Blazing torches were lowered into the kindling, and as the flames wrapped themselves around his wife's body, Orpheus stood and watched, bowed down with a terrible sorrow.

Chapter Two

The Journey Begins

When the funeral was over, when the heat of the fire had turned Eurydice's bones to fine white ash, Orpheus picked up his lyre and set off on a great journey.

He traveled for many days over land and sea until he came to a dark cave. He entered the cave and followed it down and down, making his way through tunnels that twisted to the left and right. Orpheus journeyed deeper and deeper into darkness. He waded across a river of blood. He waded across a river of tears. He passed through an orchard, its fruit sweet with the stench of decay. He passed through a forest of swords and knives.

He came at last to the edge of a dark, oily river: the River of Forgetfulness. It is the river that separates the living from the dead. Once a dead person's soul has crossed over it, they lose all memory of how they have lived and of those they have loved. On the far side, Orpheus could make out the shadowy hills of the country he was seeking: the Land of the Dead.

He stared across the water with only the thought of Eurydice in his mind. How could his lovely bride be there, in that strange dark place? He lifted his lyre to his shoulder and began to play a tune that brimmed with love and sorrow.

The beauty of the music floated out across the deep, dark water. It reached the ears of the

ferryman, Charon. He poled his boat toward

the sound.

When he saw Orpheus he said, "Stranger,

whether you are mortal or immortal, living or

dead, your music so enchants my ears that I will carry you across the water free of charge. Climb into my boat."

Orpheus stepped from the bank into the boat and the ancient ferryman pushed away from the land and poled across the river. When they reached the far side, Orpheus lowered his lyre, jumped ashore and strode into the dark shadows.

Suddenly there came the sound of growling, then a harsh barking. Out of the shadows leapt Cerberus, the great three-headed dog who guards the riverbank. He rushed at Orpheus, his hackles up, his lips curled back to show huge yellow teeth.

Lifting his lyre, Orpheus began to play again. Such was the beauty of his music that Cerberus stopped in his tracks. The monstrous dog wagged his tail and closed his six red eyes.

He rolled onto his back and howled with all three of his mouths.

Soon there was a whispering around him, a rustling, a shuffling, like the sound of the wind blowing through dried leaves. The dead were gathering. They were following him. They were enchanted by his music. It made them weep for sorrows they could not remember anymore; it made them laugh for joys that were forgotten. For the dead have lost all memory of their lives; they are a drifting host of whispering ghosts.

CHAPTER THREE

THE SORROW OF HADES

O N   A N D   O N   O R P H E U S
walked, surrounded by the spirits
of the dead. Then a palace loomed out of the
shadows, a great palace with towering black
walls. As he approached it, the dead fell back.
He found that he was walking alone. He was
approaching the dwelling place of their king.
He made his way between black gates. He
climbed steps of black stone. Doors of black
ebony swung open before him and he stepped
into a vast and gloomy hall.

At the far end of it, there were two thrones. On one sat the king of terrors, Hades, his eyes as deep as open graves, his thick beard spread across his chest. Beside Hades sat his wife, beautiful Persephone. She was like the moon shining in a dark sky, like a pale mistletoe berry in the depths of winter. It was early autumn, and she had returned to her grim husband for the chill months of winter, after bringing spring and summer to the Land of the Living.

Orpheus, still playing his lyre, walked up to the two thrones. He stood before the god and goddess. He looked into their faces. And then he began to sing,

"We mortals are wretched things,
  and the gods who know no care
  have woven sorrow
  into the pattern of our lives.
  Even the sparrow on the branch,
  even the wren in the willow
  knows more of sorrow
  than the thundering gods,
  who have never felt the cold, cold hand
  of death about their hearts.

"But you mighty gods,

though you have never known death,

you have suffered the sweet pains of love.

You have felt the piercing shafts

from Aphrodite's shining bow.

Great Hades,

imagine those long months

when Persephone returns

to the bright world above

lasting forever.

Imagine, if you can,

her pale face crumbling into dust.

That is how it is for mortal man.

Great Hades, give me back my Eurydice.

I beg you, give her back to me."

There was a silence. Then Persephone
turned to Hades, her face streaming with silver
tears. And Hades turned to his wife. One oily

black tear trickled down his cheek and splashed onto his beard. He drew breath and said, "Fetch me the three Fates."

The three ancient sisters were brought before him. The three Fates who control the destinies of men and women: one spins out the thread of a life; the second measures its length; and the third cuts it. Hades looked into the wrinkled, leathery face of the third sister. "Find the cut thread of Eurydice's life ... and mend it!"

The third sister bowed before the god and swiftly departed.

Hades turned to Orpheus. "Now go!" he said. "Leave my palace. Leave my kingdom ... and Eurydice will follow you. But never once look behind you. Do not look over your shoulder until the light of the sun shines full upon your face."

Chapter Four

The Journey Home

ORPHEUS BOWED, TURNED on his heel and left the palace. He made his way across the shadowy kingdom until he came to the river's edge.

Charon the ferryman was waiting for him. Orpheus climbed into the boat. As he sat down, he felt it tremble as though someone had climbed in behind him. He kept his eyes fixed on the shore.

When they reached the riverbank, he stepped out of the boat. Behind him he could hear footsteps, soft footsteps following him.

He journeyed through the forest, he journeyed through the orchard, he crossed the two rivers. Sometimes he could hear the snap of a twig behind him, sometimes the splashing of feet other than his own. Sometimes he thought he could feel a gentle breath on the back of his neck. Still he looked ahead.

He came to the tunnel of stone, winding to left and right. And then, at last, Orpheus was out of the cave, breathing the fresh air of the living world once again. Above him, the sky was bright with shining stars. "Soon," he thought to himself, "soon the dawn will break and the light of the sun will shine on my face."

But just behind him, Eurydice suddenly caught her foot on a stone. She tripped and she fell. Orpheus heard her stumble and, without thinking, he turned to catch her in his arms. He tried to break her fall . . . and for a single moment he saw her face, pale beneath the silver stars. Then his arms closed around empty air and she was gone.

The third Fate had cut the thread of Eurydice's life for the second time . . . and this time there would be no mending it.

Orpheus turned. He ran back into the cave, he journeyed down into darkness, he crossed the rivers, the orchard and the forest. He did not stop until he had reached the River of Forgetfulness. Standing on the riverbank, he shouted her name across the dark, oily water. But there was no answer.

Three-headed Cerberus rushed out from the shadows, growling and snarling. Charon the ancient ferryman cursed him and spat at him, refusing to carry him across. Orpheus knew he could go no further. He could not return to Hades.

So he made his way back to the living

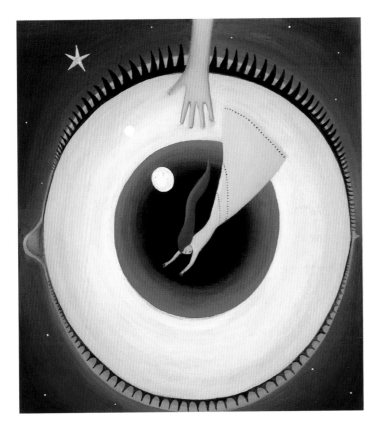

world and he devoted himself to his music,

which was more beautiful than ever, woven

through with a silver thread of sorrow. It was all

he was interested in now, all he could care for.

He devoted himself to the worship of golden

Apollo, the god of music. And he devoted himself to the memory of his beloved Eurydice.

His music was so beautiful that many women fell in love with him, but Orpheus did not care. He did not even notice their attentions. He stayed true to the memory of Eurydice and turned his back on them all.

CHAPTER FIVE

A GOD'S FURY

BUT THE BEAUTY OF HIS MUSIC also drifted up into the heavens. It reached the ears of one of the gods, Dionysus, the god of drinking and drunkenness, of madness and ecstasy, of wild dancing and wild music. He was filled with jealous rage. He cried out, "Why does Orpheus devote all his music to golden Apollo, and none of it to me?"

Dionysus looked down at the world and saw all the women whom Orpheus had turned his back on. Dionysus frowned... and with his frown those women were filled with his own jealous fury. They were maddened with a god's raging envy.

The women couldn't help themselves. They ran to the place where Orpheus was playing his lyre with the birds and animals gathered around him. They picked up stones and clods of earth and threw them at him.

But the music was so beautiful that the stones did not touch Orpheus. They dropped to the ground at his feet. So the women began to scream. The sound of their screams drowned the music, and the stones and clods began to strike Orpheus. The birds rose up into the sky. The animals fled.

Orpheus pleaded with the women to leave him alone. But they ran into a field. They found spades and sickles and the blade of a plow. They attacked Orpheus. They hacked off his head.

They lifted it up and flung it into a river. They picked up his lyre and flung it in behind.

The head and the lyre drifted downstream, bobbing in the water like apples. Then a strange thing happened. The head of Orpheus opened its mouth and began to sing. The lyre began to play of its own accord. Together they made a music so beautiful that the whole world held its breath. The trees bowed their branches and shed their leaves.

CHAPTER SIX

EVER AFTER

THE HEAD AND THE LYRE were carried by the river to the sea, singing and playing. Then they were carried by the tides and the currents and the waves of the sea. They were carried to the island of Lesbos. They were washed up on the seashore, still singing and playing.

The people of Lesbos found the miraculous head. They carried it to a cave and sat and listened to it, enchanted by the beauty of its music.

Golden Apollo reached down from the heavens and lifted up the lyre. He set it in the night sky as a constellation — a pattern of stars called The Lyre that we can still see to this day.

And as for Orpheus, he journeyed for the third time down to the River of Forgetfulness. He was a spirit himself now and Charon the ferryman was waiting for him. He was carried across the water. As he stepped onto the bank at the far side, like all the others, he forgot everything. Orpheus joined the drifting hosts of the dead.

But Persephone, the wife of Hades, saw him and remembered him. She felt pity stirring in her heart. She reached forward and touched his forehead with the tip of her finger.

In that moment Orpheus's memory returned. She touched Eurydice's forehead and she, too, remembered everything. The

two lovers found one another in that shadowy kingdom and they fell into each other's arms.

And even to this day they walk together, talking, singing and laughing. Sometimes they walk arm in arm. Sometimes Eurydice walks ahead and Orpheus follows. Sometimes

Orpheus walks ahead, knowing that he can look over his shoulder, and his Eurydice will always be there.

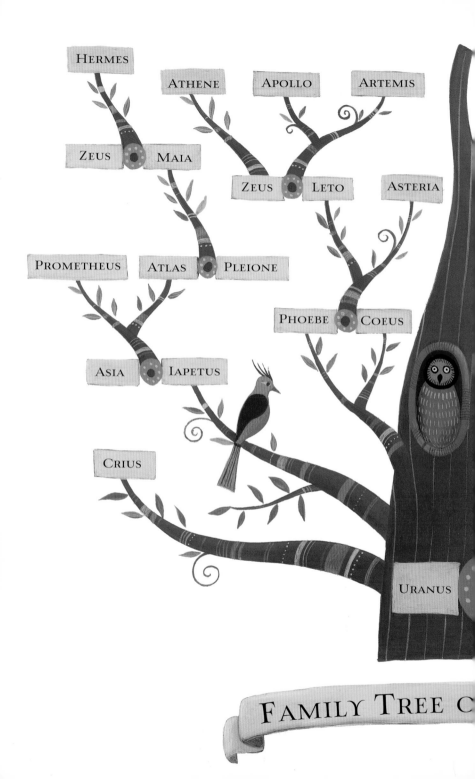

HERMES

ATHENE

APOLLO

ARTEMIS

ZEUS ● MAIA

ZEUS ● LETO

ASTERIA

PROMETHEUS

ATLAS ● PLEIONE

PHOEBE ● COEUS

ASIA ● IAPETUS

CRIUS

URANUS

FAMILY TREE C

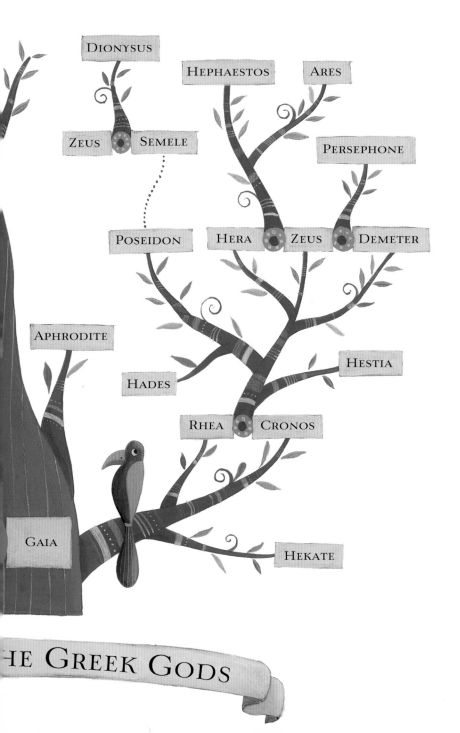

DIONYSUS

HEPHAESTOS   ARES

ZEUS   SEMELE   PERSEPHONE

POSEIDON   HERA   ZEUS   DEMETER

APHRODITE

HESTIA

HADES

RHEA   CRONOS

GAIA

HEKATE

HE GREEK GODS

ZEUS
GOD OF THUNDER

HERA
GODDESS OF MARRIAG

APHRODITE
GODDESS OF LOVE

POSEIDON
GOD OF THE SEA

APOLLO
GOD OF THE SUN

ATHENE
GODDESS OF WISDOM

DIONYSUS
GOD OF WINE

ARTEMIS
GODDESS OF THE HUNT

DEMETER
GODDESS OF THE HARVEST

ARES
GOD OF WAR

HEPHAESTOS
GOD OF FIRE

HERMES
MESSENGER GOD

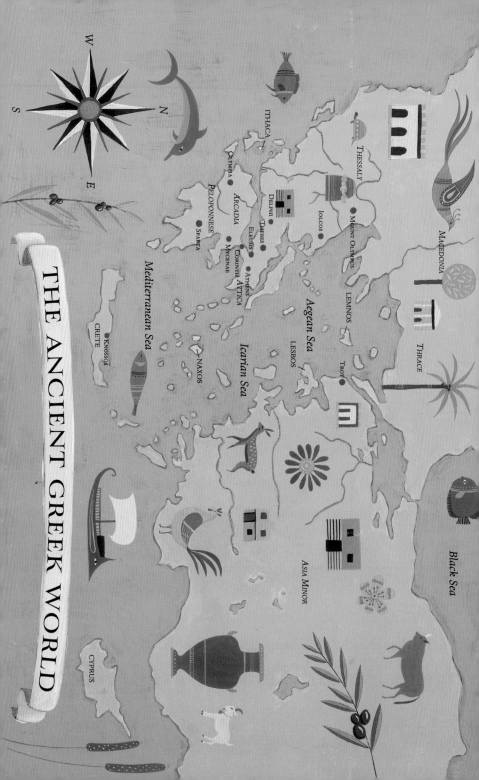

THE ANCIENT GREEK WORLD

W
N
E
S

Black Sea

Mediterranean Sea

CRETE
KNOSSOS

CYPRUS

NAXOS

Icarian Sea

Aegean Sea

LESBOS

ATTICA
CORINTH
ATHENS
MYCENAE
ELEUSIS
THEBES
DELPHI
ARCADIA
SPARTA
PELOPONNESE
OLYMPIA
ITHACA

IOLCOS
THESSALY
MOUNT OLYMPUS
LEMNOS
TROY

ASIA MINOR

MAGEDONIA
THRACE